I am so CLEVER

This edition first published in 2019 by Gecko Press
PO Box 9335, Wellington 6141, New Zealand
info@geckopress.com

English-language edition © Gecko Press Ltd 2019

Original title: *Le Plus Malin*
Text and illustrations by Mario Ramos
© L'école des loisirs 2011

Translated by Linda Burgess
Edited by Penelope Todd
Typesetting by Tina Delceg
Printed in China by Everbest Printing Co. Ltd,
an accredited ISO 14001 & FSC certified printer

ISBN hardback: 978-1-776572-48-9
ISBN paperback: 978-1-776572-49-6

For more curiously good books, visit geckopress.com

I am so CLEVER

Mario Ramos

GECKO PRESS

One gloriously sunny morning, the wolf came upon Little Red Riding Hood: "Hello, my dear! How fine you look in that delightful outfit."

"Good morning, Mr. Wolf, and thank you for the compliment," she replied cheerfully.

The wolf went on in his deep voice: "Don't you know how dangerous it is to walk all alone in the woods? You could meet some ferocious creature... like a shark! Sharks are pretty vicious, you know."

"Oh, come on, Mr. Wolf, everyone knows there are no sharks in the woods," the little girl replied.

"Of course, of course. It was just a joke. But tell me, little raspberry, where are you going with your basket?"

"I'm going to visit Grandma on the other side of the woods."

"That's a splendid idea! But what's the hurry? You're striding along as if you were late for school! Slow down and listen to the birdsong. And look at all the pretty flowers. I'm sure your grandmother would love a nice bunch!"

With these words, the wolf sauntered away, whistling to himself.

Once he was hidden by trees, the wolf ran off with a sneering laugh.

"I am so clever! I'll be having a feast today. Grandmother for the main course, and a little berry for dessert."

At Grandma's house, he knocked
lightly on the door.

Tap, tap, tap!

The door was slightly ajar and when
it opened…nobody was there.

Seeing a nightgown lying on the
bed, the wolf sniggered.

"Aha! There's an even better idea.
The little cherry for the first course…
the grandmother for dessert."

The wolf eased himself into the nightie.

"Perfect! Perfect! Disguised as a grandmother I only have to stay under the covers and wait for my meal…

"Rats! Muttonhead! I forgot to wipe away my paw prints in front of the house!" the wolf yelped as he raced outside.

Wham!

A gust of air slammed the door shut.
The wolf slunk into the woods to hide.

"Gadzooks and dogs' droppings!"
said a voice. "Oh, good morning,
Grandmother. Excuse the bad language
but I've lost my glasses. Would you
please help me find them?"

The wolf shuffled away, muttering:
"If this birdbrain thinks I'm getting
down on my haunches to help him…"

But he'd only gone a few steps when Baby Bear called out, "Good morning, Grandma! Are you collecting mushrooms for soup?"

"This 'grandmother' business is getting on my nerves," the wolf muttered, squirming to get out of the ridiculous garment.

Suddenly, peals of laughter rang through the woods.

"Hey, Grandma! Tell us if you see the wolf!" yelled Peter Pig, who was racing after his two brothers.

"Not much chance of pork today," the wolf complained.

Just then, the seven dwarfs marched past and sang together: "Morning, Grandma!" before continuing:

Hi ho! Hi ho!
Off to the creek we go.
It's far too hot
to work a lot
hi ho, hi ho, hi ho...

The wolf's blood was starting to boil even before
the Marquis Jean-Charles Hubert Hector of
Montrésor called out to him: "I say, Grandmother!
I'm looking for the castle where that beauty's been
sleeping forever."

The wolf barely kept himself from exploding as he
hid behind an oak tree.

He twisted and struggled, wriggled and writhed, yanked and twirled, but he could not take off the stupid nightie.

Then along came the little raspberry, with
a huge bunch of flowers.

"Ha! At least this one will recognize me,"
said the wolf, his mouth already watering.

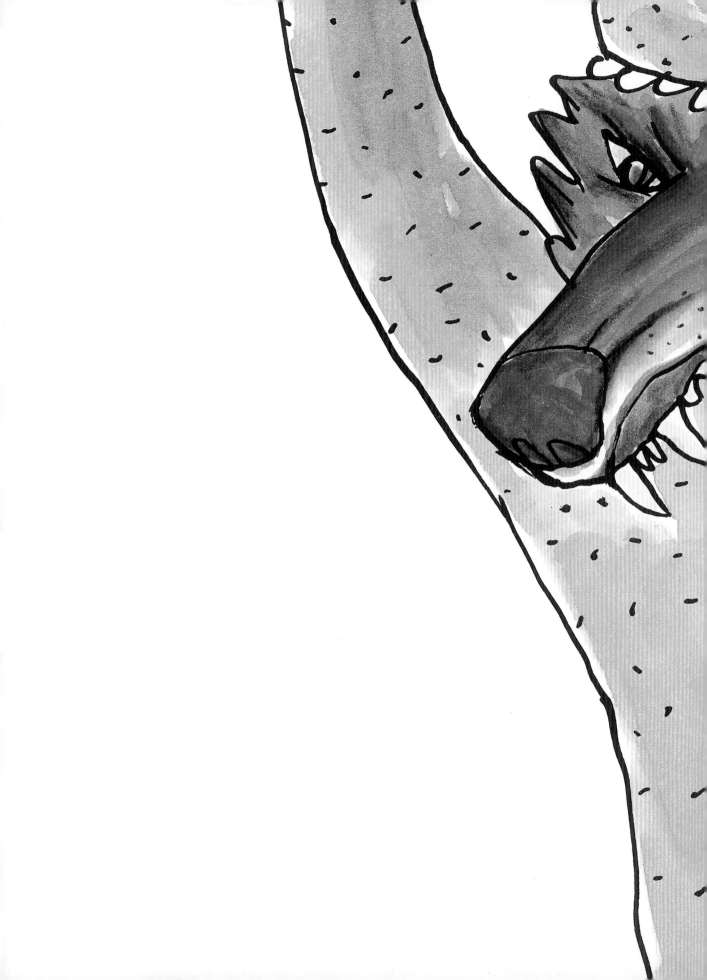

The little girl burst out laughing. "Grandma, that wolf mask is fantastic! That big furry head, those rotten teeth, the huge bulging eyes—did you do this just for me?"

Furious, the wolf threw himself at the child, howling, "I am the wolf, the Big Bad Wolf! And I'm going to swallow you whole!"

But he snagged the hem of his nightgown and crashed to the ground with an awful thud.

"Oh yes, so you are, you're the wolf! That's funny, you have the same nightie as Grandma," the little girl said.

"No iff not funny! I've broken all my teeff!
And I'm twapped in diff terrible dweff!"

"Oh poor wolf...but you mustn't get so upset.
It's very bad for you," said Little Red Riding Hood.
"Now keep still—I can get you out of there!"